Caillou®

Happy Thanksgiving!

Text: Sarah Margaret Johanson • Illustrations: Pierre Brignaud • Coloration: Marcel Depratto

chouette

Caillou is excited.
Today is Thanksgiving!
The whole family is going to
Grandma and Grandpa's house.
Caillou's cousins, Emilio and
Amanda, will be there, too.
And they are lots of fun
to play with.

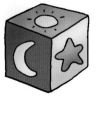

Caillou is not exactly sure what
Thanksgiving means.
But he knows he will eat his
favorite meal, turkey and mashed
potatoes. Yum! Yum!

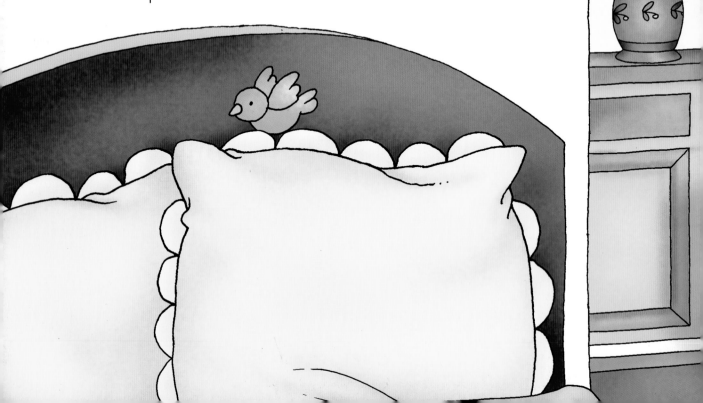

In the car, Caillou asks,
"Mommy, what's Thanksgiving?"
"Thanksgiving is a very special
day. We celebrate it once
a year to say thank you for all
the good things in our lives,"
Mommy explains.

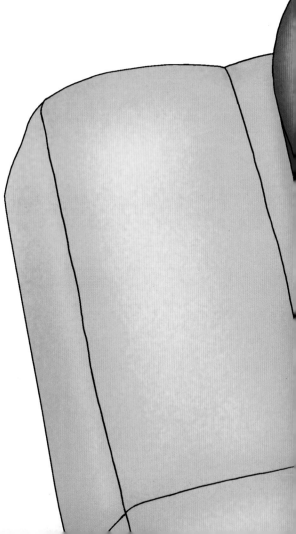

Caillou thinks about this.
"What kinds of things?" he asks.
"It could be anything
important," Daddy says.
"Like being thankful for
our great family and our
good health."

Caillou wonders about what
is important in his life.
Teddy and his toys are important.
Mommy and Daddy are
important. So is Rosie, even if
she sometimes does things he
doesn't want her to do.

Grandpa opens the door.
"Happy Thanksgiving!" he
says, bending down to hug
Caillou and Rosie.
Uncle Felix is already there.
"Hi, Caillou! Hi, Rosie!" he says,
smiling at them.

Caillou runs into the living room
and looks around.
There is nobody there. Caillou
is very disappointed.
He looks up at Uncle Felix
and asks sadly,
"Didn't Emilio and
Amanda come, too?"

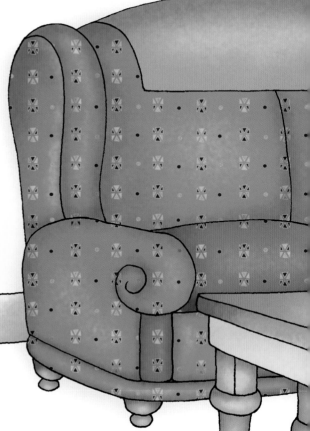

Caillou hears a little noise
and he turns around.
Amanda and Emilio jump out
from their hiding places.
"Surprise!" they shout.

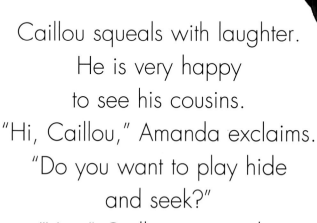

Caillou squeals with laughter.
He is very happy
to see his cousins.
"Hi, Caillou," Amanda exclaims.
"Do you want to play hide
and seek?"
"Yes," Caillou says as he
jumps for joy.

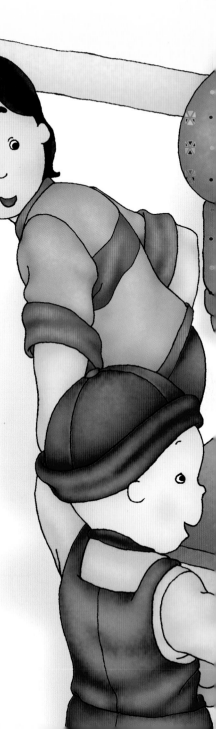

Later, everyone gathers around
the table to eat.
Grandpa asks them all what they
are thankful for today.
"Cousins to play with!"
Caillou replies excitedly
when it is his turn.

"Let's have dinner," says Grandma,
"and Happy Thanksgiving, everyone."
"Happy Thanksgiving!" they all
answer as they fill their plates.
Caillou thinks to himself,
"Yum, yum. Finally, turkey and
mashed potatoes!"

Text: Sarah Margaret Johanson
Illustrations: Pierre Brignaud
Coloration: Marcel Depratto
Art Director: Monique Dupras

The PBS KIDS logo is a registered mark of PBS and is used with permission.

We acknowledge the financial support of the Government of Canada through
the Canada Book Fund for our publishing activities.

Canadian   Patrimoine
Heritage   canadien

We acknowledge the support of the Ministry of Culture and Communications
of Quebec and SODEC for the publication and promotion of this book.

SODEC
Québec ⬛⬛

Bibliothèque et Archives nationales du Québec and Library and
Archives Canada cataloguing in publication

Johanson, Sarah Margaret, 1968-
Caillou: happy Thanksgiving
2nd ed.
(Confetti)
For children aged 2 and up.

ISBN 978-2-89718-021-8

1. Thanksgiving Day - Juvenile literature. I. Brignaud, Pierre. II. Title. III. Title: Happy
Thanksgiving. IV. Series: Confetti (Montréal, Québec).

GT4975.J63 2012   j394.2649   C2012-940526-4

Printed in Guangdong, China
10 9 8 7 6 5 4 3 2 1 CHO1840 MAY2012